Cow Under the Big Top

Text copyright © 2001 Todd Aaron Smith
Art copyright © 2001 Todd Aaron Smith

New Kids Media™ is published by Baker Book House Company, P.O. Box 6287, Grand Rapids, MI 49516-6287

ISBN 0-8010-4485-5

Printed in China

1 2 3 4 5 6 7 — 04 03 02 01

Cow
Under the Big Top

Todd Aaron Smith

NEW KiDS MEDiA

BAKER
A DIVISION OF
Baker Book House Co

One day as Cow stood in the field eating grass, she saw some beautiful green grass on the other side of the fence. Cow looked at this beautiful grass for a long time and wondered if it would taste even better than the grass on her side of the fence.

After a few minutes of thinking about the grass, Cow noticed that she was being watched. She looked up and saw a curious baby elephant looking back at her. This was something unexpected!

Cow liked elephants, but she had never seen one on the farm before! Elephants lived at the zoo! Why was this baby elephant here at the farm?

"Good morning!" the elephant said politely. "Can you please help me? I think I'm lost!" "Where did you come from?" asked Cow. "Do you live near the farm?"

"No," said the elephant. "I came from the circus. It must be far away, because I've been walking for a long time. I should go back now, but I don't know how to get there."

Cow knew where the circus was. She had heard about the circus and was very curious to see it.

Cow volunteered to take the little elephant home to the circus. She knew it would be wrong to leave the farm, but she wanted to see for herself what the circus had to offer. Cow waited until the farmer was away, and then both the little elephant and Cow left the farm for the big city.

Soon they arrived at the circus. Cow couldn't stop looking at all the lights and listening to all the interesting sounds! She had never seen anything like that!

First Cow saw an acrobat being shot out of a cannon!

Next Cow saw some trapeze artists swinging high above her!

And then Cow saw the ringmaster.

The ringmaster let out a roar of a laugh when he saw Cow! He was a very big, loud man. He grabbed Cow by the head and bellowed, "Hey! Look what I found! A COW!"

The ringmaster thought about how it might be funny to have Cow in one of the circus acts. "Imagine seeing a cow under the big top!" thought the ringmaster. Soon Cow became part of the clown show.

POW! Before she knew it Cow was hit in the face with a cream pie! The audience roared! No one had ever seen anything like that before!

Cow didn't like being hit with a pie—not one bit! But when she heard the audience's reaction, she stopped to think—maybe she did like being the star!

As time went on, Cow liked her job at the circus less and less. It seemed like all she ever did was get hit in the face with pies! Cow had had just about all she could take.

After being hit in the face with pies for the 867th time, Cow went back to see the ringmaster. She asked him to give her a different job.

The ringmaster was no longer a nice guy. He looked very angry! He did give Cow a new job, though. Her new job was to clean out all of the lions' and tigers' cages! It was a dirty, smelly job, and Cow was miserable!

Cow began to think of the farm and of the home that she had left there. "The circus wasn't such a good place to go after all!" thought Cow. "I want to go home!"

Soon Cow escaped through the back opening of the circus tent and headed for home.

On her way home, Cow began to think about all that she used to have on the farm. "I don't deserve to go back to that wonderful place," thought Cow. She was starting to feel lonely and embarrassed that she had ever left home.

"Maybe the farmer doesn't even WANT me to come back!" Cow thought. "I'll bet he really hates me now! If I ask him for a job, maybe he will let me work, just so I can stay there!"

As Cow was thinking these things, she got nearer and nearer to the farm. The farmer, who had been standing out beside the barnyard fence, saw Cow in the distance. Cow watched as the farmer began walking toward her.

"Uh-oh! Here he comes!" thought Cow. "He must be very angry with me! What will I do? What will I say? Oh, I feel so horrible!" Cow was very nervous and afraid. She knew she had done the wrong thing.

As the farmer reached her, he threw his arms around Cow and hugged her! He said, "Cow, I've been looking all over the place for you! I'm so glad you have finally come back home!"

Cow didn't know what to think about this! She knew she didn't deserve the kindness of the farmer. The farmer said, "Come on, Cow. Let me get you something to eat, then you can sleep in the best stall in the barn!"

Cow realized how much the farmer loved and cared about her. She discovered that no matter how many big mistakes she made, the farmer would never stop caring for her. As she began to eat from a yummy bale of fresh hay, she thought about how God's love must be very much like the farmer's.

Cow thanked God for his unending love. She knew it was wrong to have left the farm, but she also knew that no matter how big her mistakes were, God's love was even bigger!

Cow was finally back home where she belonged. Once in a while she thought about the circus and remembered that there's really no place like home!